True*ish*

Tales of a Non-Non-Fictional George Santos

Michael Lee Abramson

Illustrations by

Scooter Jackson

Table of Contents

Prologue

Who Did We Just Vote For?

The people of New York's 3rd Congressional District voted for a man of high moral standards. Someone who attended top schools and worked at prestigious financial firms. A descendant of Jewish immigrants which escaped persecution of both Communism and of Nazis. A true New Yorker who lost his mom because of a 9/11 related illness. A rags-to-riches industrialist who built a real-estate empire. **The people voted for George Santos!**

The real George Santos may have been anything but this person, but I couldn't stop thinking of the incredible life this imaginary George Santos must've lived. That's why I wrote this book.

The book is non-non-fiction, meaning it's completely fiction. Even the facts are fiction. As the fictional George Santos is sincere, we can surmise that his stories are true, even if the real George Santos stories are not.

Confused? Good, then you understand the premise of this book. So, with no further ado, I provide you with the life story of the George Santos we thought we voted for.

Chapter 1

Jew*ish*

"George is a liar! George is a liar!"

Despite these cries from his fellow seventh graders, George Santos stood tall and with confidence. He even had a smile on his face. This was because George recently learned a valuable lesson that some lies are actually true.

A few days earlier, George attended a friend's bar mitzvah, the third one in just the past two months. George loved everything about a bar mitzvah - the singing, the dancing, the food. He especially loved hearing the speeches, particularly the stories of ancestors fleeing from Europe with no money and becoming successful in New York.

"Hey George, when are you having your bar mitzvah?" one of his friends asked him. The question left George dumbfounded. He assumed his friends knew he wasn't Jewish. He opened his mouth to tell them of his faith, but somehow all that came out was, "It will be in July."

George arrived home that evening and was distraught about the lie he told his friends. He reflected on the past Sunday at church as the priest quoted from 2nd Peter that *'God hates the sin of lying because it is deceptive'*.

George's grandmother, who lived with him and his parents in a small apartment in Queens, sensed George was upset about something and called him over. He relayed the story to her as she smiled and told him to sit down.

"You know, grandpa and I came to America from Brazil, but we weren't born there. We were both born in Ukraine, which, back then, was part of the Soviet Union."

"What? You're a COMMUNIST?" shouted George.

"No." replied the grandmother. "We fled Ukraine and went to Belgium, where we were very happy. That is, until the Nazis came. We needed to hide our name from the Nazis, and that is when we changed our last name to Santos."

"Why did you need to change your name?" asked George. Then it hit him all at once. "Do you mean... Are you telling me we're Jewish?"

"Yes, George," replied his grandmother. "We really are Jewish. And your real last name is Zabrovsky."

"George Anthony Devolder Santos Zabrovsky," said George, wanting to hear how it sounded out loud. "Does this mean I can tell my friends I'm Jewish and I can have my bar mitzvah now?"

"George, we have followed the Catholic faith for over 50 years and your parents raised you and your younger sister that way. When you're 18 and an adult, you can decide then if you want to let everyone know you're Jewish."

George didn't like that answer and was nervous about what his friends might say of him lying about his bar mitzvah. With some hesitance, George accepted what his grandma told him, knowing that as soon as he became an adult, he would tell everyone he's Jewish.

"OK Grandma. I'll tell my friends I lied about being Jewish and that I'm not having a bar-mitzvah."

And no matter what they say, I'll smile and stand proud,
as my lie is not a lie, and that means I told the truth."

* * *

George's grandparents fled Jewish persecution in Ukraine, settled in Belgium, and again fled persecution during WWII.
- George Santos Campaign Website, Oct 14 – Dec 27, 2022

"I never claimed to be Jewish. . . I'm Jew–ish"
- Interview with Piers Morgan, Feb 20, 2023

Chapter 2

High School*ish*

George wore hand-me-down pants and a Kirkland collared shirt as he hugged his mom extra hard before leaving. It was his first day attending the prestigious Horace Mann High School. Knowing it was one of the most elite high schools in New York, George tried very hard, not just to fit in, but to exceed expectations.

As a freshman, George was quick to befriend many of his classmates, although he did not understand how their parents afforded such an expensive school. He would hear, "my mom is a doctor" or "my dad is a business executive," and George would think to himself odd that they only had one job.

"My parents work as a housekeeper, cook, nanny, house painter, and plumber," he would proudly boast to his friends.

At the start of his sophomore year, George begged his parents to buy him a jacket and tie, which many of the top students wore. As a junior, George chose finance as his area of focus. And by senior year, he was president of the after-school program Academy of Finance.

It was with only four months remaining in his final school year when everything changed for George. The stock market crashed and severely affected his family's finances. They could no longer pay the tuition. Despite his efforts to stay until graduation, George was forced to leave high school early.

On his last day at school, George was not sad or angry. He knew with the education Horace Mann provided, he would easily pass the GED and get into a great college. Upon walking towards the school exit, George paused for a moment to read the school motto inscribed on the wall one last time.

Magna est Veritas et Praevaltet

"I will dedicate my life to this motto," George said aloud.
"Truth is Mighty and Will Prevail."

* * *

"[My parents] sent me to a good prep school, which was Horace Mann Prep in the Bronx. And, in my senior year of prep school, unfortunately, my parents fell on hard times, which was something that would later become known as the depression of 2008."

– Santos on Police Off The Cuff After Hours Podcast, Oct 29, 2020

George Santos lied about having attended Horace Mann.

– The Record, Horace Mann's Weekly Newspaper, Jan 6, 2023

Chapter 3

College*ish*

It wasn't Harvard, it was better. It was Baruch College!

In the heart of the Flatiron District in Manhattan, George not only attended the college of his dreams, but he also got a chance to play in the league of his dreams: Division III Volleyball.

It wasn't long before much of the school body recognized George as he walked the halls wearing his varsity jacket. Classmates would shout to him 'Go Bearcats' and 'Beat Yale.' And beat Yale they did. And Harvard. And every other school across the northeast corridor. The Baruch Bearcat Buzz Newsletter quoted George that 'each school the Baruch Volleyball Team came up against were afraid to play against them.'

As a senior, and one week after being named to the 2010 All-Pro Team, all eyes were on George Santos. It was the playoffs, and they were on the Upper East Side at the house of their arch-rival, Hunter College.

The doctors warned George to take it easy. The years of playing volleyball at such a high level wore out his joints and he would likely need to have knee replacements soon on both knees. To make matters worse, George was exhausted, pulling all-nighters working on his final project for his Ethics In Finance course.

But he was adamant he was going to push through, as the game was not only for the championship, but it was also George's last game at Baruch. For every jump made to block a shot, the pain would punish George on the landing. For every dive to save an out, George would take a little longer to get back up. But he always did. And after splitting the first two games and forcing a tiebreaker, George pulled his team over for one last speech.

"I know everyone's eyes are looking at me," said George, "but this has never been about me. It's always been about the entire team. In my wildest dreams, I never thought I'd be playing on a sports team and have a chance to win the conference finals. And not just any conference, the CUNY Athletics Conference. But to do it, we need to play as a team. So, let's go out there and show them what we're made of."

The inspired team played an inspired tiebreaker game with teamwork and determination and upended their rival for the victory. Despite the nearly unbearable pain in his knees, it pleased George to be hoisted over the shoulders of his teammates in celebration. After all, he was their hero.

Upon graduating a volleyball legend and with a degree in finance with 3.89 GPA and *summa cum laude* honors, the school dean asked George to speak at graduation. After hobbling across the stage on crutches, George coughed lightly into the microphone, took a moment to look forward at his audience, and started his commencement speech.

"As we celebrate our achievements and mark this milestone in our lives, I'd like to talk to you about a topic near to my heart: **ETHICS**.

"In our fast-paced and ever-changing world, it's easy to get caught up in the pursuit of success, wealth, and fame. There are many temptations to compromise our values, which is why it's crucial we stay true to ourselves and uphold the highest standards.

"So, as we embark on the next chapter of our lives, it's important we don't lose sight of what truly matters. Whether it's in the workplace, in our relationships, or in our community, we must always strive to do what is right and just. Even if it means making difficult or unpopular choices.

"In closing, I'd like to leave you with a quote by the philosopher Aristotle, who once said ETHICS is the highest form of wisdom, because it requires the most delicate balance between the needs of the individual and the needs of the community."

* * *

"I actually went to school on a volleyball scholarship . . . When I was at Baruch, we were the number one volleyball team. I sacrificed both my knees and got very nice knee replacements . . . playing volleyball. That's how serious I took the game."

- Santos on "Sid & Friends in the Morning, WABC, Oct 27, 2020

"I didn't graduate from any institution of higher learning."

- George Santos Interview with the NY Post, Dec 26, 2022

Chapter 4

Mother's First Death*ish*

9/11 was just a blur for thirteen-year-old George. He didn't understand why planes were crashing into the Twin Towers at lower Manhattan. But he knew his mother worked there, and was terrified of what may have happened to her. He spent the day in the arms of his father, who tried to console George despite tears running down his own eyes for most of the day.

It was nearly 3AM when the door to the Santos' apartment opened. George, laying in his bed wide awake, jumped up when he heard the door creak. He noticed his father awkwardly sleeping on the couch in the same clothes he wore the day before and with the TV on to the local news channel. Then she appeared.

George's mom, covered in white ash, stepping through the doorway. George screamed so loud that his father rolled off the couch. **"You're alive!"**

It wasn't for another year and a half when George noticed his mother's condition rapidly deteriorate. He had then understood that the horrors of 9/11 didn't end when his mother walked through the door that night. She had advanced cancer from exposure to carcinogens from the fallen debris of the towers.

Despite costly medical bills, George's mother refused to apply for relief. "I can afford it. We're fortunate," said George's mother. "We can take care of all our medical bills. If I take funding, I'm taking it away from these men and women who need it and who put their lives on the line."

George's mother's condition continued to get worse, and just six months later, she passed away. Hundreds of people attended the funeral, including some in military uniform, which had become a custom for 9/11 related deaths.

George listened to the many speeches of how determined and accomplished his mom was to work her way from being a nanny to being an executive in just a year. This gave him a source of pride and helped him hold back his tears. The speech George remembered the most was from the funeral officiant.

"This is not the end. As her soul lives on, she, too, will live on. You will see her, hear her, even touch her, for years to come."

George's mother was in her office in the South Tower on September 11, 2001, when the horrific events of that day unfolded. She survived the tragic events on September 11th, but she passed away a few years later when she lost her battle to cancer.

– George Santos' Campaign Website: Oct 2022– May 2023

Fatima Devolder [George Santos' mom] remained in Brazil between 1999 and early 2003.

– Immigration Records received from a Freedom of Information Act request

Chapter 5

Mother's Second Death*ish*

George had no pretenses it would be easier the second time around. It was over ten years earlier when George buried his mother for the first time. However, it felt to him like it was yesterday. With the scars still fresh in his mind, George once again found himself overcome with grief as they lowered his mother into her grave.

George hosted a reception at his home after the funeral, where many of his friends comforted him. They reminded him how lucky he was to have a mother who worked long days cleaning people's homes just to keep food on the table and a roof over their heads.

One of George's closest friends tried to cheer him up. He reminisced about the times when young George would make up imaginative stories, and his mom would just roll her eyes and say, "Oh, George and his stories."

"Remember when you used to say that your mother worked her way up to become the first female executive at a major financial institution? Or when you told everyone you used to be a journalist at a famous news organization in Brazil?"

"True," said George. "I don't know why I said those things." George couldn't help but laugh alongside his friends as he was grateful for their help in cheering him up. Just then, George raised his glass in honor of his mother.

"To mom, the greatest mother anyone could ask for, may this funeral be your last."

* * *

"9/11 claimed my mothers life."

– *Tweet by George Santos [@Santos4Congress], July 21, 2021*

"Fatima A.C.H. Devolder was born on December 22, 1962
in Rio de Janeiro, Brazil to Paul and Rosalina Devolder.
Fatima entered into eternal rest on December 23, 2016."

- *Mrs. Fatima A.C.H. Devolder Obituary*

Chapter 6

Career in Finance*ish*

George got off at the Canal St. subway station and walked two blocks south before heading west towards the Hudson River. He buttoned the top button of his suit which he bought at Macy's the day before. Upon reaching Greenwich St, he stopped in front of a 39-story office tower, flaunting a clear, colorless glass façade intertwined with shiny bands of steel. It was George's first day working as an asset manager at Citigroup.

Over the years, George was very happy working there. He was well liked and built strong relationships with high wealth clients. In just his second year, he was the top seller of Citigroup's private-equity funds. George was starting to get known in the industry and after three successful years at Citigroup, George was offered a lucrative position at Goldman Sachs, which he accepted.

George worked as a project manager in their real estate division and, once again, worked hard and found success almost immediately. Just six months into his job, George got his big break. A client whom George worked with at Citigroup reached out to George with an opportunity. He was looking to build office space in the highly anticipated Hudson Yards area of New York City and was looking for an investment firm to back him.

For three months, George worked day and night on a proposal outlining how he can help with the purchasing process and negotiate a favorable deal for the real estate firm. One week later, he received the call that they had won the business. Shortly after, George was rewarded with a promotion to VP and head of a team of real estate analysts.

A second defining moment for George came just a few months later. An old high-school friend of George owned a private equity bond fund company called Waterfront State Capital and reached out to discuss opportunities to work with Goldman Sachs. George reviewed the firm's offerings and had a gut feeling they were too good to be true. He further investigated and found his instincts to be correct, as the product they were offering seemed to be part of an illegal Ponzi scheme.

Upon calling his high-school friend to ask him about it, his friend swore to George it was a completely legitimate company, but George knew better. He reported it to Goldman Sachs' ethics committee, who reported it to the SEC.

A week later, George's high-school friend reached out to understand why George felt compelled to report him. Friend or not, George knew he did the right thing and replied to him directly and ardently.

"You lied to me right to my face.
You lie to the faces of every person who would listen to you.
Lying is not a victimless crime and those guilty of lying
should ALWAYS face the consequences."

* * *

Goldman Sachs, GSAM   January 2017 to August 2017
Project Manager
New York, NY

- Private Real Estate institutional sales strategy development
- Investors Relations Client development
- 2X revenue growth from (300M to 600M)
- Developed and managed new sales strategy for the department

Citi Group   February 2011 to January 2014
Asset Manager Associate
New York, NY

- Investment orientation on LP base
- Consumer education of new opportunities
- Customer financial applications into debt and growth vehicles
- Customer management
- International customer relations

Portion of resume provided by George Santos to Nassau County Republican Committee in 2020 and as sourced by the NYTimes on 1/11/23.

Santos confessed he had "never worked directly" for Goldman Sachs and Citigroup, chalking that fib up to a "poor choice of words."

– NY Post, Dec 26, 2022

Chapter 7

Pet Adoption*ish*

"My work in animal advocacy was the labor of love & hard work."
George tweeted this proudly of his time creating and running the
Friends of Pets United charity.

George had always had a soft spot for dogs. He had frequented his
local pet store to play with the puppies up for adoption and found
this to be a great way to unwind from working long and stressful
hours. George could tell them anything, no matter how incredible,
and they would listen and be loyal to him unconditionally.

One time, while volunteering at
a fundraiser to help the pet
store raise money, George
started thinking about how can
help not just these dogs, but the
thousands of other dogs in need
in the Tri-State area as well.
That is when he decided he was
going to create his charity,
Friends of Pets United. In
just the first two months
of operation, his charity
took part in twenty adoptions.

George savored the love and loyalty he found in these pets and thought it shameful he didn't always find these same attributes in the pet owners.

As an example, after a very successful fundraiser George organized for a pet store on Staten Island, his loyalty was quickly betrayed after asking the pet store owner to write the check out to him directly. The owner rudely ignored George's request and instead made the check to the charity, forcing George to white it out and change the name on the check. George thought to himself how great it would be if the pets ran the store. They would have written out the check directly to him with no questions asked.

Another fundraiser George helped organize was to raise money for repairs for a barn in New Jersey and to have fences built for a private sanctuary for abused animals. The fund-raising event exceeded all expectations and raised over $2,000.

George explained to the barn owner that he needed time to receive all invoices of expenses before sending over the profits. However, over the next six months, the barn owner called George for the money so many times that it bordered on harassment. *'Why can't she just be patient and selfless like her pets?'* thought George.

The calls continued, and George became more and more distressed. He decided he was going to teach her a lesson in humility and no longer was he going to give her the money. That decision pleased George as the plan worked, and a few months later, she stopped calling him.

But the one person who upset George the most was also the owner of the pet that meant the most to George, an aging pit bull with a life-threatening tumor. The dog worked hard as a service pet to a homeless and disabled Navy veteran in New Jersey. George fell in love with the dog from the first time he saw his picture. With the cost of surgery to remove the tumor at $3,000, getting the money would become his top priority.

George set up a GoFundMe page and worked like an artist, posting pictures of the dog in its most crippling of states. His text was Shakespearean-like in the heroic details of the veteran dog-owner. And his hard work paid off, not just by reaching the $3,000 goal, but exceeding it.

Even as the dog's usual veterinarian in New Jersey assured George of the high success rate of the surgery, George wanted extra assurance and requested the dog to be examined by a friend of his who was a veterinarian in Queens. A few days later, George received word that the surgery was inoperable. The news was devastating to George.

Knowing of the dog owner's PTSD from his time in the military, George felt bad about adding more stress and opted to not share the news with him. Despite his best intentions in looking out for the health of the veteran by ignoring his calls, George learned several months later that the veteran reached out to state officials to take legal action against George and his charity. He thought it incredulous being treated this way for his good deeds.

Fortunately, George's good foresight when starting the charity saved the day as he had never actually registered it, for fear of exactly this kind of situation.

A few weeks later, George learned of the dog's inevitable death and went on his phone to look at a picture he took the first time he met the dog. He made sure his thumb covered the picture of the owner. After a deep breath, he thought to himself,

What a better place the world would be if humans were as honest and loyal as their pets.

* * *

Also passionate about animals and animal welfare, George founded and ran a nonprofit 501(c)(3) called Friends of Pets United (FOPU) from 2013 - 2018, an animal rescue operation, which was able to effectively rescue 2400 dogs and 280 cats, and successfully conducted the TNR (trap neuter and release) of over 3000 cats.

– *George Santos Campaign Website, Nov 2020*

The I.R.S. was not able to find any record showing that the group held the tax-exempt status that Mr. Santos claimed. Neither the New York nor New Jersey Attorney General's offices could find records of Friends of Pets United having been registered as a charity.

– *New York Times, Dec 19, 2022*

Chapter 8

Rags to Riches*ish*

In his early twenties, and like many others starting out in New York City, George had to sacrifice to make ends meet. While living in a rental in Queens, George struggled to pay his rent and his landlord threatened eviction for falling several months behind. George worked very hard to scrape together the money he owed.

Feeling accomplished for overcoming this hurdle, George withdrew the cash from the ATM as holding the money in his hands gave him further gratification of his success.

While walking to pay his landlord, a thief mugged George and took all his cash. To make matters worse, George's landlord didn't believe George was telling the truth and evicted him.

He soon found a rent-stabilized apartment in the Sunnyside area of Queens. Over the next few months, and with his financial situation unchanged, George once again could not pay his rent. For the second time in the past year, his landlord evicted him. Tired of being evicted, George decided that instead of being the renter, he would become the landlord. That way, no one can kick him out.

George established The Devolder Organization, a real estate firm, which, in a very brief time, bought and managed many rental apartments across New York City. He even had a team of brokers working for him and was the envy of all real estate companies. His accomplishments over just a few months took others years if not decades to achieve.

As things were looking up for George, he couldn't believe how quickly his luck changed as he read the Sunday morning newspaper headlines:

Orlando Gunman Kills 50 at Pulse Nightclub

Searching online and making phone calls, George's worst fear became a reality. Four of his employees, whom George knew were at the nightclub, were all shot and killed.

Overcoming this setback was difficult, however, George forged ahead and The Devolder Organization grew increasingly successful. Within a couple of years, George pulled in a salary of $750,000. Talking to a group of brokers at a real estate conference, George mentioned he could not believe how easily and quickly he went from rags to riches. Everyone seemed to agree that it was unbelievable.

George's success, however, once again took a quick turn. Along with Covid-19 came lockdowns, and many tenants found it difficult to pay their rent.

Thirteen of his tenants could no longer pay, yet George could not evict them. The newly established Tenant Safe Harbor Act prevents eviction due to Covid-19 financial hardship.

George reached out to his local representative, letting him know this law outraged him. He thought to himself that if the people don't want to be evicted, they should instead become landlords like George did.

After months of waiting and not hearing from his congressman, George knew what he needed to do next.

> **"If the government won't help,
> then it's time for me to go into politics and make the
> changes needed to help honest and hardworking
> Americans like myself."**

* * *

"My company, at the time, we lost four employees that were at Pulse nightclub."

−George Santos Interview on The Brian Lehrer Show on WNYC, Nov 21, 2022

Times review of news coverage and obituaries found that none of the 49 victims appear to have worked at the various firms named in his biography.

− New York Times, Dec 19, 2022

"I [have not received rent] on 13 properties. . . Will we landlords ever be able to take back possession of our property?"

– *Tweet by George Santos [@Santos4Congress], Feb 8, 2021*

Santos also admitted to lying when he claimed that he owned 13 different properties, saying he now resides at his sister's place in Huntington.

– *New York Post, Dec 26, 2022*

Chapter 9

Drag Queen*ish*

"No way will child grooming by drag queens be happening on my watch!" This brought George to his feet in applause, along with at least fifteen other attendees as the councilwoman from Queens concluded her passionate speech during the local assembly meeting.

George walked up and introduced himself to the councilwoman. He told her of his recent landlord issues and that he's considering going into politics to fight and change the landlord laws. The councilwoman, intrigued and wanting to continue the conversation, invited George to discuss this further at a local coffee shop.

"Progressives in this city won't be happy until every landlord is broke and every minority and immigrant can squat and live anywhere they want," said the councilwoman. "You know that most immigrants live in a better apartment than I do?"

"I believe it," shouted back George. The two spent an hour agreeing on which laws need to change and how disgusting a certain representative in northern Queens was.

"You know, George, the boundary lines for your district are changing and if you want to run for US Representative, you would have a good chance of winning. In fact," she added, "I'd be happy to support you through the process if you'd like."

That was really intriguing to George. However, the councilwoman could tell she hadn't fully sold him on the idea. "What's wrong, George?" she asked. "You would make a great candidate."

"There's something in my past which may be off-putting to voters," said George. "I used to be an addict. Not anymore. I've been clean for many years now, but I'm afraid my history will hurt my chances of winning."

"But you said you're clean now and true patriots love a comeback story," replied the councilwoman. Her uplifting tone surprised George. "Will you tell me about it?" she asked. George was normally sheepish talking about this part of his history, but the councilwoman gave him a sense of calm and trust, as if he could tell her anything.

"It started many years ago at a festival in Brazil," said George. "Some of my friends convinced me to try it, and foolishly I fell under the peer pressure. I was immediately hooked. For years, I looked forward to the next chance to meet up with these friends to do it again. I even tried experimenting on my own. But eventually I saw how much this addiction was hurting me. I took a good look in the mirror and I couldn't even recognize myself."

"The road to recovery was not an easy one," continued George, "but with the help of my family and friends, I was able to overcome this addiction."

"That's amazing," said the councilwoman. "What was the addiction? Alcohol? Drugs?" George shook his head no. "Oh, I bet it was Opioids." George, once again, shook his head no.

"I was a drag queen." The councilwoman was in amazement. "Dear god. Having the strength to recover from that, you could be president one day."

"Now when I look at myself in the mirror," said George, "I remember what I learned most from the addiction."

"The makeup and wig were just covering up the true George, and never again will I cover up what is true."

* * *

"The most recent obsession from the media claiming that I am a drag Queen or 'performed' as a drag Queen is categorically false"

– Tweet by George Santos [@Santos4Congress], Jan 19, 2023

"I was young and I had fun at a festival. Sue me for having a life."

– Santos told reporters at New York's LaGuardia Airport
as reported by NBCNews.com Jan 19, 2023

Chapter 10

Congressman*ish*

Loud cheers and cork popping erupted at the Santos Headquarters after the media announced George Santos as the US congressional winner for the Third District of New York.

George couldn't wait to get to Washington, DC. He was excited about working in a celebrated building, making new friends, and, most of all, learning what superpower he would be getting.

He was hoping for a really cool one such as controlling the future, like his favorite ex-president had. George remembered how the ex-president used his superpower at the start of Covid-19 to make the virus disappear, like a miracle, all before that Easter. Or perhaps he would get the power to change the past like the governor of a sunshiny state had used to erase over two hundred years of oppression of a race in just a few days. He figured those superpowers were reserved for more senior members and they would likely start him with something simple like the power of altering facts, which most of the more junior members received.

After just one week at the Capital, it felt like college all over again for George. Almost immediately, he was popular and known by everyone he passed. He even thought about starting a volleyball team, but figured that should wait a little while.

His fellow congressmen asked Santos to join the Science, Space, and Technology Committee, which seemed like the perfect committee for him. He even requested to lead the 'Environment' subcommittee. That job, however, went to someone with more experience in standing firm against claims of climate change. *'One day I'll get there,'* thought George to himself.

George's time to shine came just six months later. The US national debt was reaching its limit and the two parties had yet to produce an agreeable solution. George knew from his years working in finance that, if not resolved in time, there would be dire consequences for the US economy. He spent hours thinking of a solution when it finally came to him.

"Please stop me if I use too technical of a term," said George as he stood at the podium and talked into a microphone to over four hundred fellow congressional representatives. "To avoid reaching the debt ceiling, we need to demand the Treasury to issue new bonds at a high interest rate which would make it attractive to consumers. With the sales of those bonds, we can pay off the national debt and avoid reaching the debt ceiling."

"But wouldn't that just be a Ponzi Scheme?" asked a fellow congressman. George thought for a few moments and then fixed his glasses before talking again into the microphone. "Actually, I prefer to call it a Santos Scheme."

The clapping started small, then quickly spread across one side of the aisle, and then the other. Soon, every representative leaped to their feet, clapping and chanting, "Santos Scheme to the rescue!"

"I've lived an honest life."

– George Santos Interview on Steve Bannon's War Room program, Jan 12, 2023

"I have been a terrible liar.
This wasn't about tricking people. This was about getting
accepted by the [Republican] party here locally.."

– Interview with Piers Morgan, Feb 20, 2023

Chapter 11

Pope*ish*

With the world's eyes glued to their TVs in anticipation, white smoke ascended from the Sistine Chapel. There was going to be a new pope. But who?

From the balcony of St Peter's Basilica, the traditional announcement echoed around the square:

> *"Annuntio obis gaudium magnum... habemus papam!*
> *Eminentissimum ac reverendissimum dominum qui sibi*
> *nomen imposuit . . ."*

> *"I announce to you a great joy... we have a pope!*
> *The Most Eminent and Most Reverend Father,*
> *who takes to himself the name . . .*

> *POPE ANTHONY DEVOLDER"*

The new pope slowly made his way to the front of the balcony to address his faithful for the first time.

"I stand in front of you, not just as your first Jewish pope, but as your inspiration. I'm a man from humble beginnings, with parents who worked hard to ensure I received the best education. My parents also gave me the inspiration for my drive and determination, allowing me to have a very successful career in finance and in the US Congress. This experience, I am certain, will give me the tools to also be a very successful pope.

"So now, I ask of you, my brothers and sisters, let us pray."

St. Peter's Square became eerily quiet, as echoes could be heard saying, "Yes, let us pray."

Acclimating to the Vatican was not as easy for Pope Anthony Devolder as it was when he started at Baruch College or the US Capital. But he was determined to make it work, and, after a couple of years, he had reached his goal.

Talking with the cardinals in the locker room after a hard-played volleyball game, they made the pope aware of the financial issues in the Vatican. Like he had done in Congress, the pope suggested they create new debt to pay off the expenses. "Yes, we are all aware of the wonderful Santos Scheme," said one cardinal. "However, while that may have worked in America, unfortunately, it would not work here in Rome."

This was upsetting to the pope, but he knew he had the experience to find a solution. He thought hard, and soon a new idea came to him. Without saying what it was, he asked if anyone knew where he could get a dog and then disappeared, leaving the cardinals in uncertainty.

A few days later, Pope Anthony Devolder met again with the Cardinals. "I have solved our financial issues." He opened a laptop to show them a picture of himself with two sick looking dogs. Under the image, it stated:

Go Fund Me

$1,000,000 raised

The Cardinals looked from the laptop to the Pope in astonishment. "You truly are a miracle!"

www.ingramcontent.com/pod-product-compliance
Lightning Source LLC
Chambersburg PA
CBHW071235170626
46809CB00008BA/3071